NATASHA KARIS

The Initiation of Alayne Adams

To my family.
Every word is for you.

Contents

Every Initiate has a beginning. To read the story AFTER this story, and get your FREE exclusive offers, go to the back of the book for more details.

Prologue

Five students watched Alayne. For the first couple of hours, they displayed a combination of shifty nervousness and fidgety resentment. Understandable. Good. Part of the plan, even. Or had been until she discovered the note an hour ago. That *wasn't* part of the plan. Now, each one eyed her with varied degrees of hostility. Scowling impatience. Ambivalence. Or in Rian's case, with a hint of eager scorn.

These weren't your ordinary students; Alayne expected the angst and hostility from the on the cusp adults forced into this room and into this detention, but from the moment of meeting she saw a displacement. They all miss-fit, in looks or environment, in energy or body language; there was something off kilter in each person. Her initial hunch was confirmed with the discovery of the note. Someone in this room wrote of their intention to die. This meant action, drastic action. What, though? None of them were owning up and frankly it could be any of them. Alayne knew she should contact their parents or inform Principal Manning, but could she guarantee it would help once she handed the responsibility over? If she did hand over the note, the student who wrote it would never trust her. What she needed to do, was use this time to think.

For her, those years were tough, with the same contemplation. Maybe, if she delved back, she'd find the solution. The detention would run for hours yet, so she closed her eyes and allowed herself to go back in time.

1

Chapter One

They walked to the woods as day became evening, with the light still bright enough to filter through the trees. It was clear Bex knew where she was going from the way she strode, her legs tanned in microscopic shorts Alayne would never dare to wear. Although, Bex would walk like that anyway, even if lost.

'How long do you know them?' Alayne asked her friend's back.

Bex stopped and lit a cigarette. Her dyed red hair blazed with an orange frame from the light. Her eyes rimmed with kohl that ended in a huge flick at the outer corner.

'I had to do something while you were in Lanzarote,' she said as she dragged on the cigarette. 'Don't worry Al, they're cool. Remember to breathe.' She squeezed Alayne's arm and passed the lit cigarette to her, then lit another. Alayne smoked and tried not to splutter or cough this time, grateful Bex understood what she was thinking before she needed to say it.

Best friends since before memories, Bex was everything Alayne wished to be. When younger, her parents suggested she mixed with others in case their friendship waned but Alayne returned their look with a blank stare. Because no one came close, no one cooler or kinder or more fun than her. Life *was* Bex. Now fifteen, when Bex suggested they hang out with some lads in the woods, Alayne didn't question it.

They walked on, stepping onto a path of worn ground. How many people before them walked this way? How dark would this place become later? What if she couldn't find her way back? Or if she lost Bex? What if the others didn't like her? She gulped back the panic that threatened to take over because now the path opened into a clearing, with rocks and logs and six people drinking, dotted around.

'All right, Bex,' someone said.

'This is Al,' Bex said, as she sidled her long legs onto a log next to a floppy-haired guy. Who looked at her the way all men now looked at her. Alayne hovered, unsure of what to do; there wasn't enough space on Bex's log for three.

A bouncy guy bounded towards her, with his head dipped, his eyes relentless and focused, like a lion ready for the kill. He bounced right up against her, until their noses almost touched. His want to intimidate worked.

'Who are you?' His words came out accusatory, confrontational.

Alayne wanted to back away, remove herself from his scrutiny, from the anger that radiated, but she sensed it would be the wrong move. He would attack. Hostility from the others surrounded her. What had she walked into here? There was a torment in bouncy guy's eyes. A goading too. Bex was too busy talking to floppy hair to notice her panic. Alayne contemplated running, she shifted towards the way back. Her throat was closing in, the panic made the air thicker. Then bouncy guy laughed. An unexpected loud burst that made her jump. He patted her on the back and the air became normal again.

'Calm down, I'm only messing. We'll give you a go.'

An eye flicker from him to her, then to the group, hinted at a vulnerability. That little insight was enough for her to understand what he needed, to know what would make her accepted in the group. Alayne could be that person. She complied, straightened, made herself taller.

'Other way round. I'll give you a go. Until I decide if I want to stay.'

He smiled. Right answer. Banter, she would discover, was a necessity in the group. The back and forth retorts allowed the truth to slip out without putting yourself up for scrutiny.

'I'm Ross.'

'Alayne.'

'Someone pass her a can. We'll see if she can keep up.'

In the clearing, she found a rock to sit on and tried to look unfazed. She followed Bex's instructions to breathe. Right then, she realised she was changing just by staying in the woods. Already, a line crossed inside herself by being there, by taking that can. Certain she would continue to cross more lines is she stayed. She stayed under the consolation it was for Bex, because under all the confidence, the girl needed her. Bex stayed because of floppy-haired guy.

There was another reason Alayne stayed too; the fear made her feel alive. The heart thumping danger of Ross's confrontation and the scrutiny from the group gave her a thrill that still pumped around her veins. Aware they were testing her, she drank the warm, metallic, cheap liquid and vowed to prove herself. So, she stayed till the last beer drained, matching the others can for can. Whether from adrenaline or sheer determination she stayed sober. By the end of the night, the others acted as if they all forgot about the initiation. Alayne passed their test without acknowledgement.

As time went on, the groups' personalities revealed themselves until she understood the wariness that first night was just and earned, with many reasons for the way they acted. There was an uneasiness with Ross. An instability; an unpredictability. One minute he could be morose and untalkative, or argumentative and cruel. The next second he could be jumping on cars, or roofs, or them. He didn't confide in her; he kept his distance. The rumours still filtered through, of a father who used him as a human punch bag at home. Ongoing bruises proved their validity. Those early days, on one occasion when he became particularly nasty,

CHAPTER ONE

Alayne asked Sarah why they took it, why they didn't fight back. Sarah shrugged because she had no answer. After a while Alayne understood why they became accustomed to Ross's outbursts because she became accustomed too. She recognised the signs, how tension built up in Ross and when it got too much, he needed to let some pressure out. The way the group accepted his moods were a revelation, because they didn't try to change him or any of the others around them. In the group you were accepted with all your faults. Even at your ugliest.

Chapter Two

Alayne took a swig from the vodka bottle. The others talked loud *and* quiet. Some roared, while some huddled and whispered, their voices blended and echoed in the woods. She let the hum become background noise, as her melancholy disallowed conversation. Why did she even hang out here? Being around her friends was like agreeing to meet with the devil. They all skirted around danger; admittedly, part of their attraction.

Over the last three years she'd fallen in love with the others: Danny, a gangly, loud guy who made everyone laugh with his tales of weekend disasters, never causing any harm to anyone but himself. Smith, Bex's love interest, now kind of/sometimes boyfriend, was handsome and sincere with huge brown eyes; the sweetest guy, until he got a whiff of another girl. Karl, an aspiring addict, always with a spliff or a can. Jenny and Jo and Sarah and Therese; all cool girls. All working through their own disasters. All confessed to Alayne at separate times their individual problems under the promise to never, ever tell a single soul. They told her of parental problems, of eating disorders, of promiscuity. Even Bex, with all her brashness and confidence, was desperate to find proof of love after her parents' go for the jugular divorce.

In these people, Alayne discovered a different world. Another way to live. With excitement and friendship and danger amongst them. The true way, because they cared only about the important things. Forget the mundane: the bills or food shopping or cleaning or unnecessary conversations. She cringed at the false niceties her mother made as she met people on the street. Their stabs at small talk made her wince and the boredom that surged through her when she heard their words made her want to die a little. Her friends would never speak to each other like that. They lived for now. They were trailblazers. Unafraid to experiment. Fearless. They pushed their boundaries and their bodies. With them, Alayne experienced things her parents would never understand. Could never understand.

Being around them brought consequences too. Once drugs were introduced, her own life got messy. Fun times at sixteen, but they were borderline adults now, turning eighteen in a few months. This year school would unleash the class of 1995 with orders to make their mark. Studying seemed pointless and her results declined. Inevitable arguments occurred. Sunday nights spent zoned out as her parents screamed at her for not coming home the night before or, if she did, for what she was under the influence of. A big fat wedge formed, and she didn't have the wish or the inclination to deal it.

Here by the fire, accompanied with her friend melancholy, was still better than the loneliness that took over on the long, silent, nights she spent at home. Better than being alone. Still, the lads acted unhinged, even before you added anything into their systems. Was she now unhinged? After nights like this she questioned even herself.

Alayne watched as the flames licked upwards, as the oranges and reds fought and won against the air. The others gave her space, every so often sending uneasy looks her way. She'd messed everything up. Her relationship with her parents was in tatters. They realised long ago that the need to stay in bed until five in the afternoon wasn't the result of a hangover, amplified by the fact she was pale and lethargic and shaky and sore. They said they didn't recognise her anymore, and she agreed because she didn't either.

There was a twitchiness to Ross tonight, a need to poke, to provoke. Alayne could tell from the way he kept moving from one person to the next, from the constant sneer while he kicked pieces of wood into the fire and the amount he drank. From the cut above his eyebrow. His eyes locked on to Jenny who was laughing at something Danny said. Here we go.

'Hey Jenny, I heard you gave Karl scabies.'

Jenny went white. Danny looked at the ground. The hum softened, everyone afraid now to get Ross's attention.

Ross smiled with that satisfied grin he got when he found the weak spot. 'Well? Don't you wash or something? Or are you so riddled, nothing can clean it?'

Jenny's eyes welled.

Alayne had watched the budding relationship grow: the bashfulness, the blushes, the eyes lighting up as they talked to each other. Jenny and Karl finally got together last month and had been going out since. No one would say anything though, everyone was afraid of Ross when he was like that. Many eye flickers came her way.

In an altercation, she acted as a buffer or the peacemaker who the gang now depended on, which got her in trouble too. Alayne learnt the hard way that some situations you shouldn't try to talk around and should walk away from. But looking at Jenny now, who was the sweetest, most shy girl, who had finally worked up the courage to be with Karl, and Ross wanted to taint it, to dirty it and imply there was something disgusting about her. No.

'Let me think of a rhyme. What rhymes with Jenny? Or scabies? Or riddled? Or...'

'Stop it Ross.'

Alayne would give him what he wanted. A bite. A redirection. Her bad mood asked for it too. Ross's eyes watered with excitement.

'Course. Alayne to the rescue. Don't you ever get tired of butting into other people's business? Making a rhyme for you is easy. Who ever thought of your stupid name? Alayne. A lane. Your parents knew what they were doing. You're just meant to be walked down. No, walked through. And pissed on.'

She made a hand gesture to keep it coming. Ross walked nearer. Alayne was different this way; she picked up on eye movements or hand gestures or tilts of the jaw and from that deciphered their true emotion. A lot of trouble came from miscommunication. Whether between other people or from your own emotions. That was all life's altercations were. There was always a reasoning behind it all, always more than a side. Alayne picked up on what people *didn't* say. Because in the silence between their words lay the truth.

'I've got one. This one's my best yet. A lane is a pain who we piss on in the rain. Genius. Listen again. A lane is a pain...'

Ross sang the rhyme now. She distanced herself from his words knowing the more he sang the more he let go. She waited. He repeated the words in a loop, as a chant and added a dance. He got louder, gathered momentum, his movements like some ritual by the fire. He spat the words at her. Pain. Piss. Over and over.

It was fine. There was no weight in those words for her, they were just inflated, angry, pieces of hurt that he had to dispose of. Ross would relent when he saw tears or felt he won the argument or was just allowed release it, like now. His dance continued until he done what he always done. His anger fizzled out. Ross stopped. He bent and leant his hands on his knees, grinning at her in triumph. This was her chance, she could either fuel him again or calm him more.

'Remember two weeks ago, Jenny gave you the money to go out when you couldn't afford it? Or the week before, she turned up with a jacket for you because she noticed you lost yours? Or how many times she let you kip on the couch even though she knew she'd get grief from her parents? Isn't she risking it again this weekend by letting everyone come to her gaff? I think we should all treat Jenny nicer.'

Ross looked sheepish. He wouldn't fire up again, even though unpredictable, he had heart.

'Jen knows I was only having a laugh.'

Ross ran to Jenny and gave her a bear hug. Crises over. He wouldn't apologise to Alayne. That would come tomorrow or next week - not in words, but from a cigarette given if she looked for one, or an extra can, or a slip of a chocolate bar when no one was looking.

The hum began again. Alayne sat back on her log. Back to her melancholy. God she was tired.

The drugs started small, like all problems do, spliffs first, passed around the woods one night. Alayne could leave it. The marijuana made her sleepy, dozy, starving. Not a good one for a girl whose constant aim was to lose more weight. Mushies were fun. Tripping on LSD was hilarious, but you couldn't do them too often because their effects lasted much longer than the night. Flashbacks were common - still unexpected though and always inconvenient. They always happened somewhere they shouldn't, like in a queue or talking to a teacher in class and you would have to try and act normal as you felt your skin prickle, as voices blurred into each other, as faces became balls of colours that moved in waves in front of you. And that wasn't to mention if you got a bad trip. Not experienced herself, but she had been around enough friends when they slipped over the side. As they believed someone in the room would kill them, or that spiders crawled on their skin or they were dying from a heart attack. When that happened to one of the others, Alayne discovered how problem solving when you're off your head is a challenge by itself. That discovery saved her, because she never took too much like some, knowing she needed to stay on the crossroads of sanity for the pack to survive.

No, she reserved the LSD for special occasions. It was E that gripped and held her. The first time she took it, she experienced a belonging like nothing else. Full of bliss and honesty and acceptance. Everything added up, everything made sense. That first time, as she danced, it crossed her mind if she died right then, if it guaranteed her an eternity of this, it would be fine with her. The main reason she loved taking E, was instead of turning away from their feelings, people let themselves go.

No, Alayne decided, she didn't love E. She despised it because of the aftermath, because of the emptiness that descended on you afterwards. Combined with the throbbing jaws from grinding her teeth and the pain from biting the insides of her mouth. Every muscle aching from nonstop dancing. Not to mention the comedown. Actual hell. To claw a way out from the paranoia while overloaded with doubt. Torture. Then add facing her parents' disappointment and silences. Alayne hated those drugs right up to the point they entered her system and she heard a beat and loved buzzing again. Until the cycle returned the following morning when she'd feel weak and a failure.

Well, she'd had enough. Alayne stood with a slight wobble and left the rest of the bottle there.

Chapter Three

Alayne took a quick glance and ducked into the Cork City library. After the short corridor she pushed through the double doors and waved at Peter, the librarian. A world of books greeted her. The place always gave her a shiver. Not that the inside of the old library was an impressive building, just a huge rectangle of a room with high ceilings and no windows. It was the walls' of books that floored her. Under this roof, dead people's voices continued to live on, and existing author's books contained something important to discover. She ambled along the first aisle and took her time because there was nowhere else she needed to be, with all day to rummage. Alayne splayed her fingers out wide and trailed her hands along the spines of the books as she walked, touching as many as possible, in the hope some of their wisdom would seep into her fingertips. Hours were often passed here as she surrendered to other people's stories. Her favourite secret. Her friends weren't the type to appreciate setting up a book club.

Sometimes she went with a purpose to find a particular author or series. Most of all, she loved when a random book cover caught her attention and she discovered a new author who tapped into another view of life. Or the thrill she'd get when she flipped to the first page and knew from the first line she wouldn't want to put it down. Wasn't that every writers dream? To hook someone from the start, to write an unputdownable book. In the library, the world was full of possibilities.

This place transported her to different eras, other countries, or most important, another existence. The real way to time travel. Eye contact was a rarity as people came for one mutual reason; to become lost in a book.

Her eyes fell on the S's. Alayne pulled out *The Grapes of Wrath*. As she read the first line, she sighed. Here was one to sit for. She selected a chair placed in a corner and settled in. Three chapters on, with her need to read satiated, her thoughts turned to that night. It was going to be a good one, with everyone for once heading out. Alayne ran through her wardrobe options and remembered a dress she saw in a shop window. A silver zip up from that new rave shop. If she cut short her visit she could try it on, she still had money left from her birthday. Decision made she snapped the book shut and gathered her bag. As she reached the counter, she smiled at Peter, who was sticking labels on some book spines. She handed her library card to him with her book.

'Ah, Steinbeck. A classic,' Peter said, nodding his head in approval, so his flecks of grey hair moved.

'We're doing *Of Mice and Men* for the Leaving. I like his way of writing, so I thought I'd check out his others.'

'Not the cheeriest of reads, but it gives a fair representation of the time. He got a lot of flak for it from the cotton farmers, they even burned his books. But it earned him the Pulitzer. No bad publicity as they say. How are you? I haven't seen you in a while?'

Alayne couldn't tell him the truth. That she'd been too hungover or still out from the night before every Saturday for the last month.

'I'm mad studying.'

'What are you planning to do?'

'Not sure, I might just get a job somewhere. I've got till February to decide.'

'Do something Alayne, you're too smart to do nothing. The brain is a muscle. If you don't stretch it, it atrophies.'

With a tight smile she took the book.

* * *

Alayne's mother blocked the door. 'Stay in. Please. Don't go out tonight. Don't go in there.'

Alayne cursed herself. She shouldn't have worn the dress, she should have got changed at Jenny's. 'I'm just meeting Bex.'

'You're lying. Please. One of these nights something could happen. What you're taking.'

Her mother's fear irked her. It was smug, safe, judgemental. 'I'm not taking anything. I'm not dumb.'

'Well, you're acting dumb.'

'Let me out.'

'No.'

A heaviness flashed from her chest, a constriction, a need to go. 'Let me out.'

'No.'

They squared up. Alayne tugged at her mother's sleeve and when she stayed put, she tapped her arm to move. Lightly, just a warning. Her mother didn't budge. A hotness bubbled and her mother's pleading eyes done the opposite to what they meant to, because they were full of questions and disappointment. Her silence shouted, *Why treat me like this when I'm so good to you? Why treat your poor victim of a mammy like this?*

And still the stupid woman wouldn't move. Resentment rippled and turned to rage. It surged through her and almost involuntarily, she shoved her mum out of the way. As she did, her mum gripped her arm and pulled her from the door. Their shoulders thumped against the wall. Her mother whimpered in pain, but her grip tightened. The heat rose. She'd use this for days now, weeks even. Alayne tried to prise her mother's fingers away from her jacket but it was useless, the woman had clamped down. There was a need to run, to go; Alayne had to get out of here, get away. Reason abandoned her. Panic replaced it. Like a caged animal with a last chance of freedom, she lost it and put her hands to her mother's throat.

'Would you ever just leave me alone,' she screamed into her mother's face.

Alayne released her hold in horror. Her grip hadn't been hard, but it was still enough to leave a redness to the skin. The gesture was enough. It was unremovable; nonreturnable. Her mother's expression turned from fear to disgust.

'I'm done. If you go out, don't come back. I won't have a druggie daughter live here anymore.'

The only chance to resolve this was to stay. If she hugged her mother and begged her and promised to change, she could salvage their relationship. Instead, Alayne slammed the door behind her.

In Jenny's house it didn't matter if she was more quiet than usual. With five girls to one mirror, fighting to put on their makeup, the problem was trying to get a word in. They passed the vodka. She let it burn. With a plan to obliterate earlier, to forget what happened with her mother. Alayne wanted to erase her parting words, her guilt, her disgust over her actions. Tonight she would stay here, as Jenny's parents were away. A glass smashed in the next room. The lads rolled joints on the sofa. The music beat added to the excitement. Tonight would be great; she had a good feeling.

Chapter Four

Alayne was coming up. The music thumped outside the bathroom stall with such ferocity it made the walls appear to move with the beat. She placed her hand on the concrete behind her; it felt cold and clammy, but the hum tickled her palms. She slipped her feet free from her heels and let her skin take in the vibrations, disregarding the manky floor. Everything in the club vibrated. The bathroom cubicle was the best spot for the starting effects. To have a little alone time before she lost herself to the crowd and the beat. The term buzzing made sense because it was just that. Static, buzzy. Ignoring the thumps on the door from girls wanting to do the same thing as her, she sat on the toilet and examined her fingers. Her fingerprint grooves were more precise; they reminded her of vinyl records. She followed the lines for ages, with little shivers of stimulation running over her. The music warped. She gulped back breaths. Each one tasted delicious. She touched her face, smooth, exquisite. Everything was good. Now, the call of the music grew too strong.

The club was dingy, dark and dirty; nothing special. Except the music. Then the dark became cool. The dingy became a good thing, a secret thing. A special thing. And the place was hot, so hot condensation lined the roof and dripped from the beams above them. So much so that, on the floor, in that crowded place throbbing with dancing souls, the love washed over her. The house music contained a bounciness to the beat and her body moved by instinct. Alayne's senses mixed and blended, she tasted her heartbeat, smelt the excitement. Sherbet and chemical. Felt the sound as it penetrated. Her skin pores opened out and her nerves tingled to the tune. Her body pulsed in time. Scrap that, she *was* one big pulse. A pulse that joined everyone else. No differences here. Everyone came together for the same purpose, for the love of the beat and to get as annihilated as possible. Here, her brain relaxed, here she belonged.

The beat was most of the times electronic, sometimes with a vocal. Always loud. Her friends acted smug about the tunes played here, different from the so-called house music they played on the radio with the chart-toppers and sellers out. House meant underground; secret parties and dark sweaty rooms and pirate radio stations spreading the sound. House meant being awake, skinning up, experiencing life while everyone else snored in their beds.

The beat began with one style. Tonight's was a low duh-duh-duh-duh. Another faster beat joined it, more frenetic, higher in tone, stabbing the air ba-ba-bada-ba. Every couple of beats came a clash of a cymbal. A girl's voice sang, 'Yeah,' on repeat. Her voice clear, piercing, synthetic. The music Gods knew how to play it - nice and mellow at the start, building, always building to that crescendo. Too soon and the peak would dissipate. It had to be perfect. This one was a foot tapper.

The two DJ's had their own distinct taste. One preferred boppier tunes, vocals, feel-good lyrics, speaking of love, of only wanting you. The other swayed more towards instrumental long tracks that focused on the differing beats. Alayne preferred the vocals, preferred the hopeful ones. Hours were spent discussing the tunes, the mixes, the play order, the crossover between the DJ's and whether it worked. Sometimes it didn't - the record would catch or scratch, hurting your ears in an injustice to sound. Sacrilege in this place.

A shirtless guy caught her attention as he clumsily climbed onto a squatting man, until he was on top of the man's shoulders. The squatting man stood and the shirtless guy teetered left and right as he tried to find his balance. On his tiptoes and with his arms out, he jumped, grabbing for the wooden rafters that crisscrossed the club. He got lucky. His arm made contact. With unnatural strength, he pulled himself up, then onto it. On one side his head dangled and on the other side of the beam, his legs hung. The guy slid and almost fell, but his arms stayed strong and held on. Above her head, above the oblivious dancers underneath, he began to swing. Each swing became more pronounced, more confident. When he'd formed a rhythm, he let go with one arm and grabbed the next rafter. Like a monkey he moved from beam to beam. Like Tarzan if he was high. Alayne closed her eyes in disbelief, her eyes often played tricks while on something. When she opened them again, the swinger was still there. He swung the length of the room, twisted around and swung back again. Now he had everyone's attention. The room became excited, but there was a nonchalance to it too. A lot of climbing happened here. Chairs, the stage, the bar, people. The speakers at the back of the room were big; they were as wide and as tall as a person. The woofer large enough to put a foot into, which some party goers climbed onto and sat on top of, as they gurned in a drugged meditation, their delight clear on their face. No need. In the main room, the music was loud enough, anywhere you went. It slipped into you, dug into your body and sloshed around inside. They'd suffer for it later, as adults. Officials threatened the club with closure; the authorities were aware they played above normal sound levels. Anyone in the club knew this too, but they didn't care – it heightened the experience. Now mattered, not later. Climbing was common too afterwards where they would watch people scale the fountain outside the club and dance and kick the water at the crowd. Alayne witnessed one energetic guy fall from the top and crack his head on the stone lower tier. The wonder of E meant the guy jumped up as if nothing happened. Alayne shuddered as she imagined his come down the following morning.

The crowd underneath put their hands up but the guy on the beam was unreachable. This time when he pulled himself over the beam again, he lay his body onto it and lobbed his legs over either side into a sitting position. Sweat droplets slid down his face and chest. His stomach and ribs heaved. With a grin on his face, he surveyed the crowd from his superior perch. The grin said it all; he was invincible.

The music stopped, the DJ's forced to by the security now in their box, which was on the second floor and parallel to the rafters. The crowd turned from cheers to jeers. Revelation turned to annoyance. You could climb to the ceiling but you couldn't wreck their buzz. The crowd shouted various words. *Get down. Fall. Jump.*

Sweaty guy placed his hands on the beam in front and bent one leg, then the other, he looked like a frog ready to jump. He stood. The crowd shushed. For a long time he stayed still, looking down with that wide grin. Was he about to jump? The beams were narrow, his feet overlapped them. Surely he would fall if he tried to walk? The grin turned to serene determination, and he walked on the beam like an acrobat balancing on a tightrope. The crowd took a collective intake of breath. He heard it and looked down to watch their awe with glee. Sweaty guy lost concentration and stumbled. His knee banged against the beam and he fell head first. His thigh and arm caught and left him suspended above. His eyes went wide. For a moment they locked onto hers. It was as if she saw everything he was in that moment, an eternity passed between them. Alayne willed him to get up. He managed to pull himself back onto the beam. And stood. Sweaty guy shot an arm in the air in triumph and the crowd were on his side again. They roared and whooped.

'You can do it,' someone said.

'Go on. Go on,' the crowd chanted, Alayne included, over and over, until they made their own music.

Sweaty guy began to walk. Unsteady and slow, with his arms

outstretched like anchors he made his way along the beam. Each step brought him closer. The room became silent. Sweaty guy became more confident, got faster, until he broke out into a run. There was only a few more steps. Alayne's heart quickened. As he neared the DJ box, multiple hands shot out and grabbed him. They pulled him, launching him head first into the safety of their arms. His feet were the last part to disappear. A hush came over the room. Sweaty guy's bravery rewarded him with a visit to the elite. To the gods; their DJ's had welcomed him into their embrace. The bouncers would beat him afterwards, that went without saying, their toughness a necessity in a place like this. But it would be worth it. For that moment, sweaty guy was untouchable.

The music started and everything kicked in. Louder, faster. Her high expanded to another level. A whoosh ran through her. The pulse pulsed stronger. The energy in the room thickened like a fog. Alayne danced, matching the beat.

In the crowd she found some of her people. Bex smoked in the far corner, her head against the wall with her eyes closed. Smith sat on the bench next to her, as his eyes rolled while he rubbed Bex's leg. On the other side of the room she spotted Danny, who danced now like a maniac. She loved that guy. The others were in the back room or out in the courtyard. Jezzer walked towards her; he was the biggest dealer in there, but cool. Everyone was cool. His eyes locked on, intent on her. Not what she was after. She turned and danced in the other direction, weaved through the many jerking bodies, to create some distance. All good. The music changed to a favourite. She moved nearer to Danny to say hi, but too many blocked the way. The crowd whooped and bounced higher. Some even jumped now. Alayne joined them and the song lifted her; she wanted to go higher, to touch the roof. Nothing was impossible, sweaty guy just proved it. She stretched her hands above her head, as high as they would go. As muscles and sinew pulled further outwards, as every cell inside felt the stretch, she became more. Pure pleasure erupted. Alayne stopped jumping and rocked her hips and let her body sway. Her laughter travelled over the pumping music. An arm went around her waist, warm and safe. All cool. Everything is when you're on E. As she glanced again in Bex's direction, her friend returned her stare. Bex looked worried. Weird. Someone nuzzled her neck. Jezzer was the nuzzler.

The room shifted sideways. Jezzer wasn't cool. Jezzer was vicious. You didn't say no to a guy like him. A coldness ran over her. Not all right. She'd heard stories about him; stories of a girl and two kids. Stories that he also beat the girl, hospitalised her last time. Not boyfriend material. How would she get out of this? Fuzzy brain blocked rationality; her natural instincts off. Act as if you're out of it, she thought. Blame it on the drugs. She laughed and patted his back and went to walk away. Everything would be fine.

Jezzer caught her hand and pulled her back. He made a pronounced lick on his lips; his tongue on thin moustache gave her a shiver of revulsion. Jezzer noticed. He threw her hand away as if it burned him. Her arm hung by her side, she stared at its floppiness, her brain slow to process. Jezzer spoke and brought her back.

'Slag.'

What could she say to rectify the situation? 'I can't, I'm with someone,' she said.

Jezzer leaned in. 'And that would stop me?' He caught hold of her arm, digging his thumb into her skin hard enough to tip bone. 'I'll have you if I want you.'

The place changed. The music ripped through her ear drums and the beat she loved a minute before, threatened. The dark now scared her. In a room full of dancing people, she was helpless. With everyone out of it, they wouldn't even know or care if Jezzer pulled her out of the club. Or threw her down on the floor. Or slit her throat right in front of them. Alayne heard other stories about him too.

21

That's the thing about E. It shot you to the highest point, lifted you until you couldn't go any further, and then came the turn; the shift, and you woke up on the edge of a cliff and the only way down was to get on your ass and shovel through the muck and manure and scrounge through the dirt and thorns. That, or jump to your guaranteed death.

The shift was here.

Bile travelled and gathered in her throat. She swallowed it. If she tried to talk, she'd vomit. Alayne backed away.

'You think you can make a show of me?' Jezzer flashed teeth now. His fangs punched his lip, like a dog about to bite. A hand appeared on Jezzer's shoulder.

'Gillie's down outside. Baseball bat,' the hand owner shouted.

Jezzer pointed at her, then made a fist, as if to strike. 'You wait,' he said, then shoved a dancing guy out of his way, and another, until he disappeared into the throng.

Alayne ran to Bex's now empty corner and vomited. Images distorted, everyone now a blend of shapes and particles that broke up and moved. Here was the turn; the downer on its way. No sign of Bex, or Smith or Danny; maybe she imagined them. The music distorted, assaulting her brain, the sound came out broken up, disjointed.

Get out now.

The words came out clear as a moments logic drifted by. Jezzer would wait for her outside. Or worse, come back in. The only other way out was through the hotel that joined the club. But that was a no go. Locked. Her only hope was Ray. The crowd now a swarm of moving colour and mocking sound. She shuffled the short distance, concentrated on one foot after another, until she reached the pit - a circular bar with a suspended mesh fencing that pulled down if things got raucous, which they often did. The barman's face moved and shifted. In an attempt to fix her visual vertigo, she shook her head. It gave a brief reprieve to lock down Ray's eyes, his worried expression told her he knew. She didn't speak, knowing anyone might hear, anyone might report back. Everyone wanted to be on Jezzer's side. Instead she let her eyes do the talking. *Get me out of here. Please.*

Ray opened the hatch of the pit and walked with his head down, weaving through the bouncy, smiley bodies. The place now looked like a small budget horror film. Once her crowd, now they seemed stupid, resembling oblivious, screwed up, eye rolling, ridiculous expression, zombies. At the end of the room, Ray inserted a key inside the lock of a hidden black door, opened it a fraction and moved aside.

'You tell John I said ring a cab OK?'

'Thanks,' Alayne said.

Ray nodded, then pushed her through the door. The bang as it closed made her jump. An empty, cold corridor faced her. The absence of the roasting room made her damp clothes like ice against her hot skin. The noise of the club muffled, distant, but far from safe. She needed to hurry. At the end of the corridor she came to stairs. She cursed her heavy heels as they clanked on the metal steps. As she looked down they disintegrated into particles as small as sand. Colours streaked in front and blurred her vision. Her eyes were useless now, only touch could help her find the way. Alayne tried to not freak out, as her heartbeat raced, with the taste of vomit in her mouth, as shapes and colours zigzagged in front of her. She clung to the stair's railing and tapped the ground with her foot to find the edge. The steps were unending. She began to think she would never get out until she touched concrete floor. Flat and welcome. Two doors blocked her path. The signs wouldn't stay still, the letters chopped and hopped around. She shook her head and opened her eyes as wide as they would go. Still nothing. She pushed the first door and made out a broom with her hands. Not that one then. The second door opened into a wide space. A man with hair that swayed and eyes on his cheekbones touched her arm. 'Ray rang down already. I've a cab booked.'

John guided her to the seat as if the black circles instead of eyes, the grinding jaw, the guilt and the trouble, were nothing he hadn't seen before.

Her skin spiked, different to the pleasant sensation before. Each prickle now like little pins stabbing her. For the first time, the spiders came crawling for Alayne. With none of her friends to talk her round. She let her paranoia run. Jezzer would be outside. Or Jezzer would be in the cab. Or John and Ray called Jezzer and he'd walk in here any minute. Or he would find out where she lived and break into her house and kill her. Jezzer ran that place. Even if none of that happened, how could she ever come back to the club?

'Cab's here,' John said.

Chapter Five

The remnants of the night became a creeping, barefoot nightmare as she paced and rocked in her bedroom. She could barely form words for the cab driver. With effort she managed to give him her address and then Alayne let the world spin for the rest of the journey. She took her shoes off outside the door and twisted the key as quiet as she could because a confrontation with her parents would be too much. The stairs were easy, the creaking steps memorised so many times she could avoid them even while sleepwalking. On the painful comedown, she wore headphones to silence her noise inside.

As night became morning, Alayne examined her features in her bedside mirror. Her cheekbones sunk into arches. Her skin exquisite only hours ago, displayed a variety of yellowed dry patches, flaky now. Her hair hung in greasy clumps from sweat. Colour had vacated her face, as if all life and blood drained from its surface leaving her like some drugged out vampire. Gnawed down swollen lips. Insomniac black orbs for eyes. She hated the person that looked back. So she dug her nails into her skin and dragged them along her arm. Everything about her was disgusting.

The pain helped.

No more. No high was worth this shaky, weepy, fragile horror. She would stop going to the club, stop taking drugs, right her mistakes with her parents, with school, with herself. Become Alayne again. Appeased enough to attempt sleep, she walked to her bed and lay and closed her eyes and welcomed the fitful, jagged slivers of unconsciousness.

As the day became evening, the reception in the kitchen was caustic. Her mother sat at the kitchen table with her back to her and stared out the window. By the angle of her head tilt and the way she straightened her back, her mother expected war. Alayne hugged her from behind and handed her a ceasefire.

'Last time, I promise.'

Her mother slumped her shoulders. 'Nothing I haven't heard already.'

'I never promised before.' Alayne's voice was hoarse. It hurt to talk with her chomped on the inside cheeks.

'To promise, you would have to admit you done something.'

'I'm sorry. For last night. For what happened yesterday. Everything, I'm sorry for everything.'

She sidled into the opposite chair and let her mother see the wreckage. She wouldn't hide the damage anymore. Her mother winced.

'I was going to pack up your things today.'

'One more chance, please.'

Her mother's mouth made a line. 'You need to stop hanging around with those friends. I don't want you going to the woods anymore. No more going to those places, no more drugs.'

'Anything,' Alayne said.

* * *

Depression descended on her those first few weeks, followed by the paranoia that left her terrified to go outside her front door. Her thoughts ranged from manic to calm; one day delighted with her achievements, other days running through ways to kill herself. Torturous and unstable.

She kept to her word and didn't go out. Just in case she slipped up or ran into Jezzer, she didn't go anywhere but school. On her good days she questioned herself. What had she done so wrong to him? Those days she reasoned, she wasn't that important to Jezzer, he would have forgotten all about her.

In the night though, sometimes right before sleep, a coldness crept over and she would know, her and Jezzer weren't over.

To keep busy, she studied and read. Her parents allowed her one thing; her friends could call to the house. Every ring, every knock on the door disappointed her because it was never the people she hoped for. Bex was never the caller. Alayne missed her friends. Missed the banter and the million things going on at the same time. The lack of drama left a gap, a hole, an emptiness. The group often spoke in the early hours of a party about the missing man. Even in a room full of everyone you knew, there was always a feeling someone was missing while you were on E. Sitting in her room, alone, night after night, it dawned on Alayne what it was, the only missing person had been her.

Bex disappointed her. Their friendship, or what it needed to survive, unveiled itself. Now that Alayne was forced to do something different, she was surplus to requirements. Bex wanted no one but Smith. A splintering happened, with no argument between them. Around school they acted the same, yet an underlying uneasiness spread. The unsaid of her not hanging out at night, fractured her from the group. They avoided her. The distraction of her friends problems and the naivety that they cared as much for her was replaced with an unshakeable void. A sadness accompanied her wherever she went. Life now was just study, school, sleep and reading. It sucked.

That first Saturday night, she sat in her room and drank vodka. Her parents had asked her to watch a movie, but she couldn't bear the silence in between the ads that screamed of how broken they were as a family. The more the alcohol went down, the more convinced she became of her failures. Each sip brought more guilt, more shame. Her family would never trust her again, would never look at her with love again. The damage was irreversible. None of her friends cared about her anymore, not one of them had called. Had they ever cared? Everything was ruined. Life was so bland now. Nothing excited her. Nothing seemed worthwhile. The only thing left was her, Alayne, and she despised that person.

An overwhelming need to hurt herself took over. At the mirror she clawed her face. Smiled at the scratches and the red welts. The satisfaction only lasted a minute. As her reflection drained the bottle, she had never hated anyone as much. It would be better for everyone if she ended it. Alayne tore at her drawers to see if there was anything to harm herself with; looking for a scissors or anything sharp. There was a belt. In a few minutes it could be over. She wrapped the belt around her neck and looked for a high spot. The wardrobe bar. A calmness took over, a resolve, a rightness, which convinced her more it was the right thing to do. She opened the wardrobe door and stepped inside. Reached for the bar. Wobbled. The floor inside was uneven, sending her off balance. Her sister's teddy.

Her sister.

Her sweet four-year-old sister who still looked at her as if she adored her. Who had no idea what a screw up she was yet. This wardrobe was her favourite hiding place. An image flashed of Cara's glee when Alayne made a loud deal of searching, of how she would hear her giggles from outside the room. How would her sister react tomorrow? Who would find her? Who would be the first to find her dead in the morning?

She couldn't do it to them, she had hurt them enough. Instead she sat in that wardrobe and cried. Alayne cried until the skin on her cheeks were sore. She cried until all possible tears and spit and drool left her. She cried with that belt still around her neck. When she could cry no more she staggered into bed and undoing the noose, she let sleep take her for a moment from her misery.

CHAPTER FIVE

* * *

As she jumped off the bus, she adjusted her heavy bag of books. The trip to the library, once another highlight of her week, was now the only thing she looked forward to. Done for distraction those first few weeks, they became her saviour as she gained strength from the characters she read about. Every one of them taught her something else. The latest book was *The Virgin Suicides* by Jeffrey Eugenides, a new favourite, the angst of the girls related and mirrored hers. Their boredom she understood. A gem of a find. The title drew her in; the story hooked her. The discovery of a new writer unveiled itself with a new version of the world so well written she smelt the surroundings, felt the emotions.

So it was with excitement that she pressed the button for the pedestrian crossing. As she crossed, a guy, shifted position on the opposite side of the street, outside the high metal gates of the park. Even hunched over with his head down surrounded on either side by two shifty looking guys she could tell who it was. It felt like her body was about to turn to liquid and drain down to her toes. The hotel that backed onto the club was a couple of doors down from the library. What was she thinking coming near on a Saturday? How stupid of her not to think that Jezzer might start selling early. She considered walking back but thought better of it, to turn in his eyeline would draw more attention. She scurried on, praying and making silent deals with God.

Whether from the beeping of the crossing or the bunch of people nearing him or the fear that emulated from her, something caught his eye and Jezzer's head flinched in her direction. Half way there. The library was right next to the park; the sanctuary of it called to her. If she was lucky, she would pass unrecognised; with her hair scraped back and no makeup, a different girl crossed the road from the one in the club. Dressed down, she may go unnoticed. Or as she reasoned before, he may have forgotten all about her. Not too fast to trigger his interest, she took strides towards the entrance, but couldn't help a glance, to check he hadn't seen her. He had. Jezzer moved fast, with the other two following. Alayne moved faster.

'Get over here,' he shouted.

One building separated them. Alayne pushed through the door. Jezzer, his voice louder now as he closed in. 'Stop her.'

As the door shut, she sprinted through the empty corridor because if Jezzer caught her there she would be alone with nowhere to go. After pushing the double doors of the main library, she strode past the counter hoping to hide behind an aisle. Hoping if Jezzer couldn't see her, he wouldn't follow. Peter saluted her but his smile turned to confusion when she didn't stop. His nose wrinkled at the commotion coming from outside. Jezzer and the two guys smacked the doors open so hard they hit the shelves on the other side. The books wobbled and a few slapped down onto the floor. Alayne froze mid walk, exposed in open space.

'Outside. Now,' Jezzer roared loud enough to startle a man reading; his newspaper motioned like a Mexican wave.

As she turned to face the man who consumed her nightmares, Peter made a stop gesture with his hand, then he strolled towards Jezzer as if a lunatic stood on the opposite side of the counter was normal. 'How can I help?'

Jezzer made his resident snarl. Away from the safety of the dark, Jezzer's features frightened her more; his eyes were more ruthless, in the light his thin nose and thinner moustache were more rodent-like. There was a recent addition to his face - an Indian ink tattoo of a teardrop by his eye. Wasn't that a sign you killed someone? The jittery way his eyes moved and how he stood with the balls of his feet rocking told her he was using what he dealt too. He leant over the counter, so he was almost touching Peter.

'Keep out of it you. This one owes me.'

He shoved a pile of books towards Peter for effect. Peter didn't flinch, which angered Jezzer more, the snarl now so forceful, blood should pour from his lip.

'Do you want a book?'

Jezzer's mouth resembled a fish sucking its final breaths. He turned to the guys on either side of him, then laughed, fake and forceful. 'Hear yer man?' His laughter stopped, he eyeballed Peter. 'Do I look like I want to read? Get her out now or I'll wreck the place.'

Jezzer stepped towards her. Alayne stepped back.

Peter made an exaggerated sigh. 'That's what I thought. I don't want any trouble. The girl is a customer and doesn't want to go. Leave or I'll call the guards.' Peter picked up the phone from its cradle and hovered the hook near his ear. 'Your decision. I'm sure you'd love to spend the evening in Bridge Street. I've a friend there who would be happy to comply. They like a bit of a warm up during the day to get them in the mood.'

Bridge Street was a Garda station notorious for beating the people being held there. Peter's threat worked. Jezzer bit down on his lips for maximum threat but at the same time walked backwards, with the other two following, until the doors swung back and closed.

Those doors were the only way out.

'Come through,' Peter said. He opened the hatch on the counter and gestured for her to follow. Drama over, the other library participants returned to their books. With shaking legs, she followed Peter into a small room; the space allowed a table, two chairs and a worktop. Books piled as high as her hip tiered along every wall on the floor and every available surface of the worktop. Peter turned on the kettle and made her tea, adding two spoons of sugar.

'I don't take sugar,' she said.

'It's for the shock.'

Peter, up close, looked younger. It was only his calm ways that added years. There was a quietness to him; a maturity, a holding back in order to listen. A tenderness in the way he handed people their books.

'I'm sorry I came in and caused trouble.'

'Seems to me you weren't the one causing it.'

'Yeah but they followed me, if I hadn't come here they wouldn't have started.'

Peter handed her a steaming cup, she let the heat warm her shaky hands.

'I'm glad you did. If you went somewhere else, he may have hurt you.'

'I don't know what to do. He isn't someone to mess with. It's not about money, I embarrassed him which is way worse. I've tried to avoid him. Stopped doing the things I shouldn't. Tried to be better. I gave up everything, my friends, the club, my life and he still found me. And nothing's changed. I thought staying away would help me, but I'm still… lost. Nothing got better,' Alayne tried to breathe. 'He won't let it go, he'll wait outside all night for me.'

'I'll give you a lift home.'

'We won't even make it to the car, he'll have ten guys outside.'

'There's a private car park underneath here for staff. Let him wait outside all night. You won't be here.'

'You'd do that?'

Peter's eyes narrowed. He took a while to answer. 'For something in return.'

Disappointment shovelled over her. Another guy wanting a piece.

'Would you help me here some days? We're backlogged with books as you can see. I can't pay that much, but it would look good in a job interview if you worked in the library.'

Alayne broke out in a smile, her first in weeks. 'Are you serious? You don't even have to pay me. That would be my dream job.'

'OK then, you get a half day on a Wednesday?'

She nodded.

'A lift now for work on Wednesday afternoons.'

'Done.'

For the second time, Alayne sneaked out a back entrance to avoid Jezzer.

Chapter Six

It surprised Alayne how much satisfaction came from the methodical work of alphabetising books. She loved everything about working in the library: the silence, the respected mutual concentration, the chance to read in quiet moments. Most of all she loved the smell; the scent of knowledge wafted into her. Now with free rein, she saw the other parts of the library she hadn't noticed before, as she had always gravitated to Fiction. She slotted a book into the Philosophy section, an area that terrified her.

Peter brushed past her holding a pile of books, then stopped and placed the pile on a table nearby. Beside her he scoured the titles.

'Here we go,' he said, selecting a particular book and handing it to Alayne before walking away. 'Recommended reading. Part of the job requirement.'

Alayne read the title of the thin book. *As a man thinketh* by James Allen. She read the inside page.

'Mind is the Master power that moulds and makes,
And Man is Mind, and evermore he takes
The tool of Thought, and, shaping what he wills,
Brings forth a thousand joys, a thousand ills:—
He thinks in secret, and it comes to pass:
Environment is but his looking-glass.'
'OK.'

'Come back to me when you've read it,' Peter called back.

Alayne sat on her break drinking coffee and read: *'The soul attracts that which it secretly harbours; that which it loves, and also that which it fears'*

What did she harbour? Did she love anything? Books. She definitely attracted plenty of them; as soon as she finished one, another story excited her. Fear she knew well. Her biggest fear had been bumping into Jezzer. Had she attracted him? She read on.

'Good thoughts bear good fruit, bad thoughts bad fruit,' she said.

'Every thought-seed sown or allowed to fall into the mind, and to take root there, produces its own, blossoming sooner or later into act, and bearing its own fruitage of opportunity and circumstance.'

She stopped. The words didn't even go in; it made little sense to her. Same with the next. The words jumbled around. It was impossible; the book was too old, it hurt her head to concentrate, the drugs had fried her brain. Alayne threw the book on the table in defeat.

'Well?' Peter asked, as he entered the room and pointed to the closed book. He sat next to her and opened his lunchbox.

'A lot got lost if I'm honest.'

'Alayne, you can do better than that.'

'I'm telling the truth. The words made me dizzy.'

'So, less than thirty pages defeated you. What *did* you take from it?'

'Nothing.' She stopped talking. Instead, she thought for a minute. 'What you think about plants a seed and grows. If you have good thoughts then better thoughts grow, if you think bad, you get worse.'

'Sounds to me like you grasped enough.' Peter picked up the book and flicked through until he selected the page he wanted, then read aloud. *'"Good thoughts and actions can never produce bad results; bad thoughts and actions can never produce good results. This is but saying that nothing can come from corn but corn, nothing from nettles but nettles."* You get that right?'

'Yeah. When I hear the words from you I understand but reading from the page, it twirled in front of me.'

'We'll read it out loud then. Here's a good one. *"Suffering is always the effect of wrong thought."'* Peter placed the book on his lap. 'What have you been thinking about Alayne? Can you see the line you've been following?'

She met his eyes. He returned her look with no judgement. Peter picked up the book without waiting for her answer. She didn't listen to the rest of his words, instead she brought up the many thoughts she told herself. They were not good.

He caught her attention by waving his hand in her face. 'Here's my favourite: *"He who cherishes a beautiful vision, a lofty ideal in his heart, will one day realize it."* I love that.' He closed his eyes and savoured it, then handed her back the book. 'Take it away for the week. Read a page at a time, a line a day if needs be. Study the words until they make sense.'

As Alayne walked home from the bus stop, she pulled out the book from her bag and repeated the words as she walked. *'Cherish your visions; cherish your ideals; cherish the music that stirs in your heart, the beauty that forms in your mind, the loveliness that drapes your purest thoughts, for out of them will grow all delightful conditions, all, heavenly environment; of these, if you but remain true to them, your world will at last be built.'*

She took it slow. Repeating sentences until each one sunk in.

Each morning when she woke she didn't do her usual scramble out of bed. Instead, she lay and dreamed. What did she want? To drop the shame and guilt. To feel better. To be loved. To love.

Each week Peter handed her a new book and they would speak of the previous one on their lunch break. He introduced her to new authors: Napoleon Hill, Earl Nightingale, Joseph S. Benner.

The book piles in the library kitchen became personal. Any free moment she took a couple from the top and categorised the obvious. The not so obvious she read and at the end made a judgement on where they should be placed. Alayne didn't tell anyone the real reason those books were so important - that if she could find a place for them, maybe she would find she had a place too.

'Any more problems with that guy?' Peter asked one day on their now regular coffee break.

'Nope, haven't seen him but I don't go to the places I used to either. Every time I come here I still check outside but he's never around. Course, I don't come on a Saturday anymore. I try not to think of him. When he crosses my mind I try to flip it. I imagine him forgetting me or him giving up drugs. Or I replace him with a different thought; I picture me a year from now in university, doing well, walking to class with a great big grin. It works. I feel happier and I like that because I don't want to be the person I've been. I don't want to dislike myself anymore.'

'Good for you.'

In that big room, Alayne absorbed and learnt. No subject was off limits. Biographies on great people. Art workbooks with techniques practiced at home. Books on body language and behaviour, on love and life patterns. From them she began to understand the warranty of feelings. Of the indications, like pointers, that could show where you were in your head. What with study and her own assigned curriculum, every available moment Alayne craned in a book. On the way home Alayne bought ingredients from recipes that caught her eye from the cookbooks sifted and salivated over. Then had fun as she experimented that night. After, she presented them to her family; some worked, others didn't. One particular time, as they tucked into chicken supreme, the creamy sauce indulgent and comforting on a cold day, her mother gripped her hand. With no words used and no need for words; her mother's hand told her how thankful she was for that dinner, but more so, for her daughter's return.

* * *

'What did you make of it?'

Alayne handed Peter back the book called *The Greatest Thing in the World.*

'At first I thought you gave me something that preached from the Bible, but it wasn't at all. Like, when he wrote about Judgement day and how the final test of religion isn't about religion. It isn't about how or what you believed but how you loved. That made sense to me, because I never understood how any religion can make you feel unworthy. Or that if you've lived your life with kindness you could still go to hell because you picked the wrong team. When Drummond wrote, *"God is love,"* it got to me, because that was always the way I imagined whatever created us should be.'

'Exactly. It says, *"Where love is, God is."* There's a difference between spirituality and religion. You can believe that there is something more without following religious rules or customs. Although, for some, there is comfort in that, in having a place to pray or belong. The book says if you have faith but no love you have nothing. That love is greater than faith. It's like where Drummond says, *"We love because he first loved us."* Something created us; something loved us enough to make us. What stood out for you?'

'That if you live your life with love, if you put it first before anything else, then there is no need to worry about anything. Everything stems from love. It made me question how little I put out there. I've spent nights thinking about my relationships, my mistakes. The friends. The people that came into my life. Where I went wrong. The lessons they taught me. That's how I see them now, each friendship, each argument was a lesson. For a long time I was really sad that all my friends disappeared. It hurt, but I don't blame them anymore. We were an accumulation of lost souls. We hoped as a collective we could piece each other together, but the jigsaw parts didn't fit. Even the Jezzer situation. It forced me to stop. I needed something to, or I would have got worse until something worse happened. They all led me to now. Sorry, I went on a bit.'

'Not at all.'

'Instead of looking for something or someone to take away my pain, I had to find something I liked in me.'

Peter's eyes crinkled as he smiled. 'Love. The Greatest thing in the World.'

* * *

Saturday nights were very different from before. Movies replaced drugs. Parents replaced dancing friends. Films gave Alayne the opportunity to find a way back into the sitting room, back into her parent's lives. On the ad break, her father got up from the couch.

'Snack time. Who wants one of those new fancy biscuits?'

'They're for visitors or special occasions,' her mother said, attempting badly to scold.

'What could be more special than watching a good movie and having our daughter cuddled up to us. Huh?' he said walking into the kitchen.

Her mother slipped her hand into Alayne's. 'True.'

That was her moment, to say the things that built up. To open up all that was unsaid.

'Mum, I'm sorry. There can never be enough sorry.'

'Shh,' her mother continued to watch the screen but squeezed her hand.

'No I need to say this. I've been reading a book that says love is made up of nine things. I didn't practice any of them. I wasn't patient. Everything had to be done right away. It's why I was always panicky, because I didn't trust the things I wished for, could happen. Another is kindness. I haven't been very kind.'

'Al.'

'Please mum, listen. The next one is humility, I thought I was above it all. And there was so much anger in me and I wouldn't even know at what. I looked at life all wrong. I didn't show you much love.'

Her mother placed her other hand on top of their clasped one, her eyes threatened tears. 'We knew you loved us. We always knew that. It was you, you didn't love. And we didn't know how to make you. You are so different, you were always so different.'

'I know, I've never fit in.'

'Some people aren't meant to. Did I ever tell you the story of when my mother died? Not her death, I mean what happened straight after. I was in the bathroom upstairs when I got the call. It was sudden, and my mother had been everything to me. I was devastated. For a moment I had to place my face on the cold floor just to stop myself from fainting with the shock. But you were so young, only three, I couldn't leave you on your own downstairs. And I didn't want you to get upset; I wanted to shield you from every possibility of pain. So, I put on a fake smile and sat on the couch. You were playing with some blocks on the floor. You took one look at me and left what you were doing and climbed onto the couch. You stood next to me, your whole self only reaching the top of my head. You stroked my hair. Gentle strokes over and over. When I looked into your eyes, I saw such kindness and understanding. You hugged me and all the false brightness left. All I could do was let the tears go. Alayne, you just knew. You knew exactly what I needed. I think the drugs were just a way for you to try to be the same, to take a break from being so good to everyone. For a minute to fit in but some people aren't meant to. It's part of you to help people. That's a gift.'

The doorbell rang.

'I'll get it,' her father shouted. After a moment, he shouted again, 'Al, it's for you.'

40

Her mum gave her hand another squeeze.

Bex looked pale and different; sheepish. Alayne folded her arms. The red dye in Bex's hair had grown out with only a hint on the tips, returning the rest to her natural brown. She wore none of her trademark eyeliner either. Her bare face made her look younger, more vulnerable. Alayne resisted the urge to hug her.

'Let me guess. It's over with Smith.'

Bex nodded, made a circle on the outside mat with her foot.

'You better come in,' Alayne said, stepping out of the way. 'Upstairs. I don't think it's a good idea for my mum to come out to you.'

In her bedroom, Bex fiddled with the jewellery box, fingered the photo frames, avoided eye contact.

'Why are you here Bex?'

She examined one picture. 'I miss you,' she said. Her voice came out quiet and awkward.

'You didn't miss me when you had Smith. Or when I bawled my eyes out in my room. Alone. You could've called round.'

Bex looked up with a pained expression, 'I wanted to, but you know what Smith's like. He was always breaking it off, I knew if I didn't meet him, he'd go off with someone else and now it doesn't matter because I lost him anyway and made a fool of myself.'

'What happened?' Alayne tapped the bed. Bex smiled at the allowance. She sat.

'Saturday night, down the woods, Ross was on one. Starting on everyone. Called Danny a fool, an embarrassment. Mocked Jo about her spots, Sarah over her teeth. He kept taking our stuff and dangling it over the fire. Wanting a rise you know? But none of us would react, we know what he's like.' Bex's eyes flicked to hers, Alayne nodded to continue. 'So he got worse, nasty. Called me a slut and said everyone thought it, even Smith. I told him to go away.' Her voice caught. 'Smith said nothing. I knew by the way Ross grinned there was something coming. He said, "Two sluts sharing, right Therese?" You should have seen Therese's face, the way she went puce and kept her eyes on the ground. Smith wouldn't face me, but he laughed. Laughed. Jo's eyes couldn't hide it. I flipped. Caught Therese by the hair and tore her onto the ground. They had to pull me off her. Turns out they've been going behind my back the whole time. Therese didn't even say sorry. All the girls said nothing, acted like I was the one in the wrong. I'm done with them all.'

'Sorry.'

Bex caused her much pain these last few months, but she wouldn't say anymore. The words in the book made more sense now, *'Love cannot be provoked.'* Her mother's words stuck too. Bex needed help. At the end of it all, everyone wanted the same thing. Love, in some form.

Bex ran her finger along a crease in the bed sheet, 'I'm the one that's sorry, I should've stopped hanging around with them when you did. Deep down I never trusted Smith. I've been a sucky friend. There were times when something would happen, and I would want to tell you and remember you weren't around. I missed you. It never felt right when you weren't there. You seem happier Al. I want that. I'll do the same as you, get my head down, sort my life out.'

'I've been reading about the difference in trying to please and giving pleasure. I've always tried to please. By sacrificing something of myself. To make people like me, I guess. One book I read says being kind gives the most pleasure. I want to try volunteering or something. Maybe down the homeless shelter. Would you come with me?'

'I'm in.'

Bex took a relieved breath. They both knew she'd forgiven her. Time to change the subject.

'The club's turned to shit anyway. Did you hear about Jezzer?' Alayne shook her head, she'd told no one except Peter about what happened. 'The club got raided, just as he was stashing his gear in a vent he'd cut

42

out. They found loads. Some people thought he got out way too quickly. A lot of heads were after him, paranoid he'd squeal. The Doyle's said he was a dead man if they found him. Talk is he ran to England when he got out on bail. There's been war since between the Doyle's and the Kelly's. Fights most nights. Raids. They're talking about closing the club.'

'Crazy,' Alayne said, but inside she was popping champagne corks.

Chapter Seven

Alayne handed Peter a coffee at the counter.

'Last day,' he said, taking a sip.

'Last day,' she said.

'Well, Alayne, it's been a pleasure having you here.'

'It's been fun. Thank you for everything. The books you gave me, they should teach them in schools.'

'Wouldn't that be something?'

'Teaching's down as my first choice.'

'Good for you. Exams next week?'

'Yep. Maybe it's too late, but I've studied. Done everything I can. I was a good student before the other stuff got in the way.'

'I wouldn't doubt you for a second. What type of teaching?'

'Secondary. Teenagers, for sure. Because I've made the mistakes, I've tried the wrong things, had the head wreck, the confusion. Maybe I can help them because of that. I hope anyway,' Alayne beamed at Peter. 'For a long time, the good inside me peeled away until I couldn't remember any positives. You helped me see I'm all right. If I can be half as good a teacher as you, I'll be happy.'

Peter beamed back. 'I've enjoyed this. Each book I gave you, reminded me of the lessons they once taught me.'

A man walked towards them carrying a pile of books.

'This is Sean Adams. The new guy that will take over from you. He's just moved here. Give him the rundown Alayne.' Peter winked at her, then pivoted and disappeared into the back. Strange. Sean unleashed the pile of heavy books he struggled with onto the counter. There was a feeling in the pit of her stomach. Not bad, not good either. More a recognition; an awareness to take note.

'Hi,' he said.

'Have we met? You look familiar.'

'No,' he said, as he furrowed his brow. His black eyelashes were so long they curled. 'I'd remember.'

She blushed, changed the subject. 'Moved from where?'

'Knockfarraig.'

Alayne lifted half of the pile on the counter and moved them closer. 'Knockfarraig?'

'It's about an hour's drive from here. The town's small. But it has a long beach with a bandstand and it's full of hills so there's some cool views.'

'Sounds nice. You should show me there some time.' She stopped. Was she flirting?

'I will.' Curly eyelashes fluttered at her.

'So why move?'

'Because I don't want a life with regrets.'

'Me too,' she said.

It wasn't instant love. There was more a compelling. To learn more, to be around more, to pursue the conversation. A difference in how Alayne felt as she spoke to him. Because of him. She smiled back at the man who would later become her husband.

* * *

Alayne's eyes snapped open. Years had passed again and she was back in the room with the students. Who were still fidgety, still resentful.

Even though everything changed for her.

She thought about what she learned from Peter and what she'd taught herself with the books she'd read since. About the lessons she'd planned to teach and never got to. About what had turned her life around and how it nearly didn't. What she learnt about love from Sean and what she'd forgotten along the way. This time, the student's resentment didn't daunt her. Instead, Alayne was excited. Because now, she had a plan.

Get your exclusive offers here!

I send out an occasional newsletter with information about giveaways and new releases and glimpses of my life as a writer. As a thank you for joining, here's what you will receive for free:

The Summer Before

Since her mothers death, Calista's life has been a struggle. Convinced romance is the answer, she is desperate for someone's love. Not from any guy though. She only wants Finian and will do anything to make him fall for her. But if Calista gets the love of her life, how will she manage to keep him? Read Calista's novella BEFORE she met Alayne. Discover how she ended up in the detention room and became one of The Initiates. (You won't find this anywhere else!)

The first chapter of The Initiates

Free eBook of As a Man thinketh by James Allen (Featured in The Initiation of Alayne Adams)

Free eBook of The Greatest thing in the World by Henry Drummond (Featured in The Initiation of Alayne Adams)

Get your Initiation pack at: https://www.subscribepage.com/thesummerbefore

Enjoy this book? You can make a difference.

Honest reviews of my books help bring them to the attention of other readers. If you enjoyed this novella, I would really appreciate if you could spend a few minutes leaving your feedback. Reviews help the buyer understand the 'feel' of the book so your review could be the difference in whether someone picks it up.

My deepest thanks,
  Natasha Karis.

About the Author

Natasha Karis is currently putting the finishing touches to her second novel *The truth between us*. Her novel *The Initiates* and *The Happiness Initiative* (the free practical exercise eBook included with *The Initiates*) are out now.

Reading and family are her passion and when she isn't writing, she can be found with a book in one hand and a child in the other.

She lives in Cork, Ireland.

Her online home is www.natashakaris.com

Connect with Natasha:

on Facebook at natashakarisbooks

on Instagram at @natashakarisbooks

Also by Natasha Karis

The Initiates
'A wonderful, uplifting tale'
'captivating'
'life-affirming'
'It truly touched my heart'

Five lost students. A suicide note. One teacher who will stop at nothing to help them.

Teacher Alayne Adams loves nothing more than to help. So when the Principal of her school in Knockfarraig, a small town in Cork, Ireland, suggests a series of detentions for some wayward sixth year students, she volunteers. But the discovery of a note reveals one student intends to end their life. When she questions who wrote it, there is silence. Alayne has no choice but to take action. Taking inspiration from a book based on ancient teachings, Alayne embarks on a series of life lessons that encourages each of them to discover ways to heal their pain. Can she steer them onto a path that will change all their lives?

Includes a link to the free eBook The Happiness Initiative, a practical exercise book based on Alayne's teachings.

The Happiness Initiative
TIRED OF BEING CONTROLLED BY YOUR EMOTIONS? ARE YOU
UNSATISFIED WITH THE LIFE YOUR LIVING?

Discover ways to shift a negative emotion. Learn how to work up the
emotional poles. Figure out what it is you really want. This book uses
practical exercises to help you get to the heart of what makes YOU
happy.

These are Alayne's further teachings.

JOIN THE HAPPINESS INITIATIVE TODAY!